KANATA CLASSICS

From McClelland & Stewart, one of Turtle Island's oldest and most venerable literary imprints, comes KANATA CLASSICS, a ground-breaking collection that proudly brings together significant works of fiction and non-fiction by Indigenous and non-Indigenous voices to create a new conversation and to lead the literary discourse on the multifaceted nature of this country, its culture, history, and identity.

The Kanata series champions brilliant, timeless books that push the boundaries of literary excellence, and challenge our existing understanding of Canada to reflect the rich and diverse range of voices in our country.

Launched in 2025 to mark the 10th anniversary of the Truth and Reconciliation Commission Report, the series welcomes First Nations, Inuit, and Métis writers—historically excluded and miscategorized—to the literary classics space. Inviting writers from across Canada's many identities, geographies, and generations, each book features commissioned introductions and stunning cover art culturally connected to each author.

All titles are carefully selected to bring a balance of Indigenous and non-Indigenous voices into provocative and nuanced dialogue with one another, putting our literary culture to the work of true reconciliation.

Eight-year-old Ahsinee could hardly wait to visit her grandparents and spend the entire summer in their little log house by the lake. Every night, as her Mooshoom puffs on his pipe, she asks him for a story. "Now, my girl," he asks, "what is it you want to know?" This time, Ahsinee asks for the story of fire, and Mooshoom tells the story of Little Badger and Grey Coyote.

When Mother Earth was young, both people and animals spoke one language. A young blind boy named Little Badger is guided by Grey Coyote, who shares his teachings about the interconnectedness of the world they live in. But Little Badger's people are desperate for protection from the long, cold winters, so Grey Coyote guides the boy on a daring adventure: to find the Fire Spirit in the heart of a mountain and bring warmth to his people.

Works by Maria Campbell

BOOKS

Halfbreed (1973; 2019)
Achimoona (1985)
The Book of Jessica (1987)
Keetsahnak/Our Missing and Murdered Indigenous Sisters (2018)

CHILDREN'S LITERATURE

People of the Buffalo: How the Plains Indians Lived (1975)
Riel's People: How the Métis Lived (1976)
Little Badger and the Fire Spirit (1977)
Stories of the Road Allowance People (1995)

PLAYS

Flight (1979)
Jessica (1982)
Uptown Circles (1984)
One More Time (1995)
The Alley (2001)

FILM

Edmonton's Unwanted Women (1968)
The Red Dress (1977)
Sharing and Education (1985)
Road to Batoche (1985)
Cumberland House (1986)
A Centre for Buffalo Narrows (1987)
My Partners My People (1987)
Joseph's Justice (1994)
La Beau Sha Sho (1994)
Journey to Healing (1995)

OTHER

Campbell, Maria. "We need to return to the principles of Wahkotowin." (*Eagle feather news* 10.11,2007)

Campbell, Maria. "Foreword: Charting the way." *Contours of a People: Metis Family, Mobility and History* (2012. In B. Macdougall, C. Podruchny, & N. St-Onge (Eds.), Contours of a people: Métis family, mobility, and history, (pp. xiii–xvi). University of Oklahoma Press.

Campbell, M. (2017) "Blankets of Shame" In. L. Charleyboy, Lisa, and Mary Beth Leatherdale, eds. *# NotYourPrincess: Voices of Native American Women.* Annick Press, 2017

Neissen, Shuana. *Shattering the silence: the hidden history of Indian residential schools in Saskatchewan.* Faculty of Education, University of Regina, 2017.

Campbell, Maria, et al. *Keetsahnak/Our Missing and Murdered Indigenous Sisters.* (Edited by Maria Campbell et al., Edmonton, The University of Alberta Press, 2018)

LITTLE BADGER AND THE FIRE SPIRIT

Maria Campbell

ILLUSTRATIONS BY Kate Boyer

Introduction by The Author

Kanata Classics
McClelland & Stewart

McClelland & Stewart hardcover edition published in 1977
Kanata Classics edition published 2026

The authorized representative in the EU for product safety and compliance is Penguin Random House Ireland, Morrison Chambers, 32 Nassau Street, Dublin D02 YH68, Ireland, https://eu-contact.penguin.ie

Library and Archives Canada Cataloguing in Publication
Title: Little Badger and the Fire Spirit / Maria Campbell, Kate Boyer ; introduction by Maria Campbell.
Names: Campbell, Maria, 1939- author. | Boyer, Kate (Illustrator), illustrator.
Description: Kanata classics edition. | Series statement: Kanata classics | Illustrated by Kate Boyer. | Previously published: Toronto: McClelland and Stewart, 1977.
Identifiers: Canadiana (print) 2026011765X | Canadiana (ebook) 20260120057 | ISBN 9780771023507 (softcover) | ISBN 9780771026263 (EPUB)
Subjects: LCGFT: Picture books. | LCGFT: Fiction.
Classification: LCC PS8555.A535 L5 2026 | DDC jC813/.54—dc23

Cover design by Kelly Hill
Cover and interior art: Kate Boyer
Kanata Classics logo by Luke Swinson
Typeset in Village by Arthur Dennyson Hamdani
Printed in Canada

McClelland & Stewart
A division of Penguin Random House Canada
320 Front Street West, Suite 1400
Toronto, Ontario, M5V 3B6, Canada
penguinrandomhouse.ca

1 2 3 4 5 30 29 28 27 26

For my children,
Roxanne, Tanice, Daniel, and Cynthia—
"the four little drums who helped a blind lady
see a whole universe"—
thank you.

GLOSSARY

Ahsinee	Stone Her name is Red Stone Woman.
Kookoom/Nohkom	Grandmother
Mooshoom	Grandfather
Ma-he-kun	Wolf
Waa-hi	Exclamation i.e., Good Gracious
Mas-cha-can-is una	He was a coyote, that one.
Ni-kis-kis-in aqua	I remember now.

INTRODUCTION

By Maria Campbell

"Nohkom, where did we get fire?" my grandson asked, climbing up beside me on the sofa. "My teacher wants to know, and here is my gift for the story." He handed me a small tobacco tie and a jar of homemade jam. "Me and mom made the jam," he said proudly.

This was the first time I had ever received tobacco and a gift for a story, so it was very special. I was not a very old nohkom then, and only real storytellers and old kookooms received tobacco and gifts, or so I believed. I was very intimidated. I didn't know where our people got fire. I had heard many stories, but I never heard that one, so I began researching.

I talked to my father and went wherever I knew Elders might be gathering, offering tobacco and gifts to all the people who I thought might know. But no one knew the story or remembered except an old aunt, who didn't remember the story, but did remember that it was a little blind boy who brought us fire.

"I'm sorry my girl," she said. "I know lots of stories about fire, but I don't know that one. Maybe you should call Uncle Smith, he has a good memory, and he is also an oskahpaywis, which means a helper to the old men. He must know."

Well, Uncle Smith must have known I was thinking about him because he called me that night and when I told him what

I wanted he chuckled. "I am taking three Elders to a culture camp in the mountains," he said. "We are leaving in the morning. Why don't you come with us as a helper at the meeting and later in the afternoon you can speak to the old people who will be there and ask them if they know the story."

So off I went to the culture camp. One of the Elders we travelled with was an old woman who was not only a storyteller, she was also a pipe carrier and a Knowledge Keeper. I was thrilled to be with her. In those days, the early 1960s, I didn't know many elder women who were storytellers, much less pipe carriers. Those kinds of things, even ceremony and some stories, were kept very quiet. Nobody talked about them because it had only been a few years earlier that our people could go to jail for smoking a sacred pipe or telling sacred stories.

Maybe that is something you could research. Google it or find books in the library that tell stories about that time. There were a lot of things that our people couldn't do for a long, long time. Like not being allowed to speak our language or practice our religion. It's very interesting and an important part of Canada's history that everybody should know.

Anyway, going to the culture camp with those old people was a wonderful trip. I learned so much and those Elders became my teachers and were just like family. But they didn't know the story. Lisa, the old lady Knowledge Keeper who was travelling with us, suggested that I create a story using what I had learned so far, and they would help me by sharing all the elements that would make a good story and be culturally true. Not a tahp achimowin, a true story, or an ahtyokayiwin, a sacred story, but rather it would be an achimowinisis, a small story written for a book.

"We will be your advisors and helpers and you can write it," she said. "Then your noosimis, your grandchild, will have a book to take to his teacher and his school."

So that's what I did, and those old people helped me by sharing teachings and stories about fire with me. They encouraged me to use my own life experience as background for the story and that's what I did. I grew up in the bush and I had a mooshoom and kookoom just like Ahsinee, the little girl I created for this story. And my mooshoom and kookoom would tell me stories about all sorts of things: about animals like musqua, the bear, and piyasisuk, the birds; about the Thunderbeings and why the seeseepuk, the ducks, waddle when they walk.

Well, I started to write. I had the first draft done in a few weeks. One day Jack McClelland, who was my publisher, came to Edmonton and I gave it to him, but he said, "No, I want you to read it to me." And so I did, and he said, "I love it, Maria, and I will publish it, but I would like three more over the next three years."

I was so excited I could hardly wait to tell the Elders that I had a publisher. They were so excited and moved. "Awe me!" Lisa said clapping her hands. "I knew it would be a book! I could just feel it in my bones."

And that evening after I had read it to them, we had a celebration with a feast of pemmican and dried Saskatoonberry soup. Maybe in the next book I will give you the recipe. It's very easy to make and it's very, very, yummy.

●

Little Badger and the Fire Spirit is now thirty-nine years old and is being reprinted with illustrations by a new artist, my dear friend Kate Boyer, whom I've known since she was a little girl and whose art I started collecting when she was about six or seven years old. I have known her for nearly all her life. She comes from just up the river road from me. We both live on the banks of the South Saskatchewan River. I have been admiring Katie's art since she was a little girl, so when the publisher decided to publish a new edition, I asked Kate if she would do the art and she agreed, and I love it. Her work is gentle like my mooshoom and nohkom and like our homeland. Thank you, Katie.

I thank her for her beautiful and gentle art, and I thank also Denise Bukowski for guiding me through this and Stephanie Sinclair at McClelland & Stewart for reprinting this special edition and my great-grandchildren and their teachers. I hope you love the story as much as I do.

Little Badger and the Fire Spirit

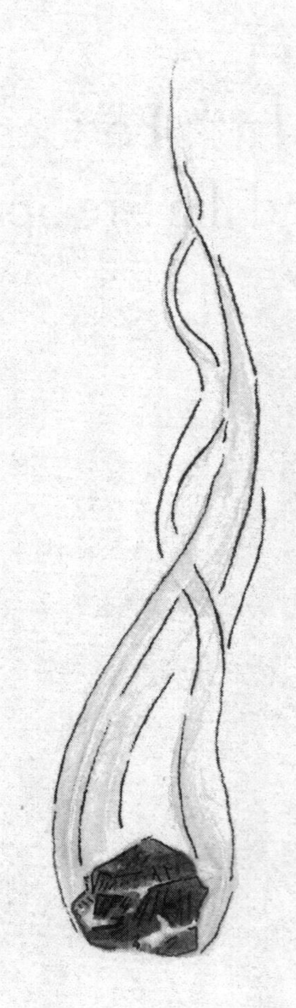

Ahsinee was going to visit her grandparents, Mooshoom and Kookoom. She was so happy she could hardly wait to get there. It was her eighth birthday and for a present she could spend the whole summer with them.

How lucky could a little girl be!

Mooshoom and Kookoom lived in a little log house right beside a huge lake called Lac La Biche.

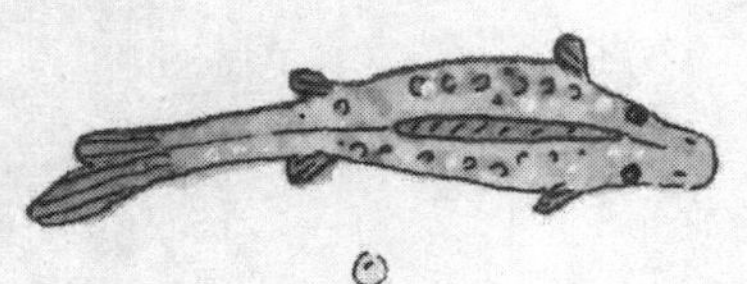

Here Mooshoom spent his days mending nets for the fishermen who fished in the big lake, and making snow shoes for the trappers who went far into the wilderness to trap when the first snows came.

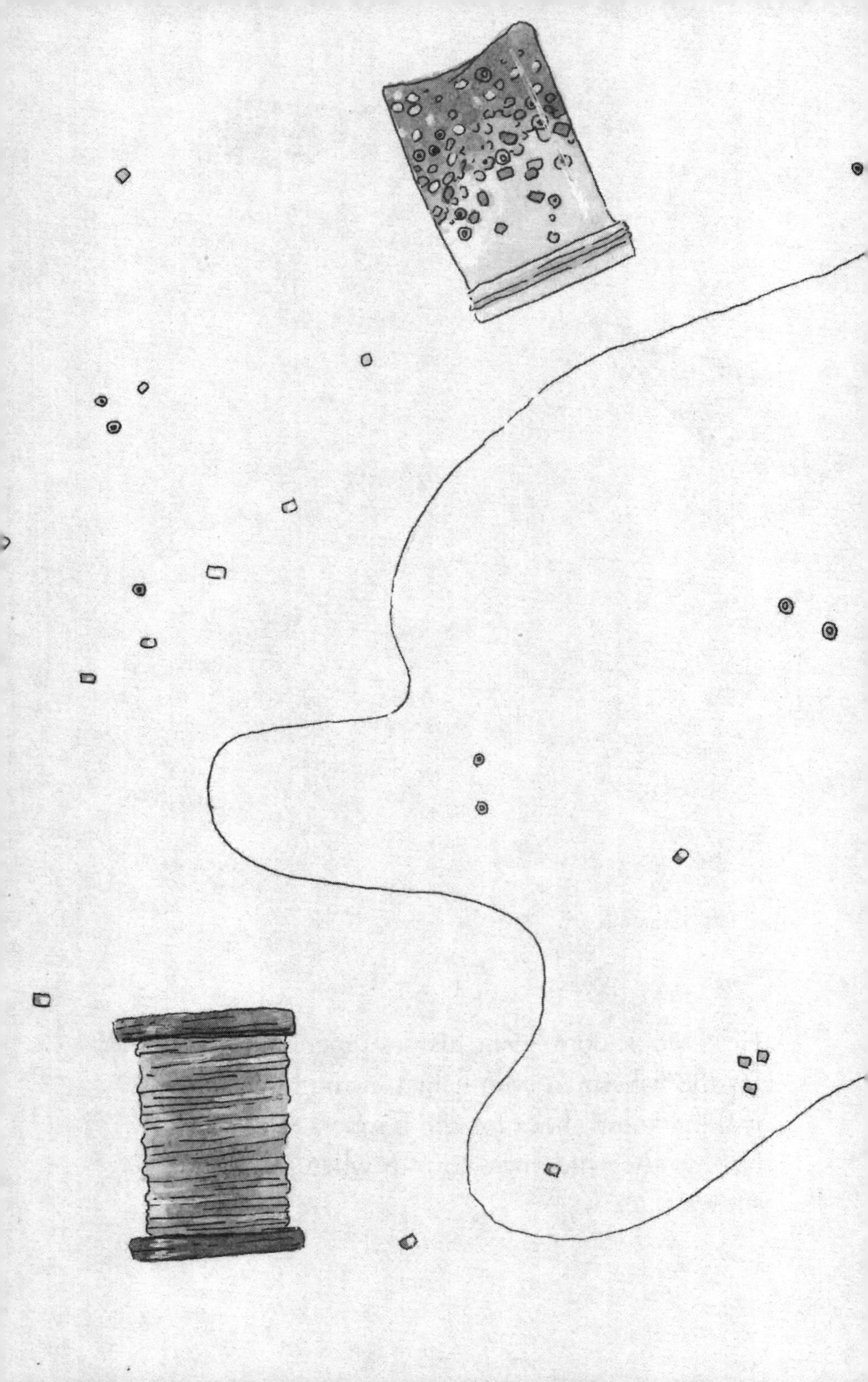

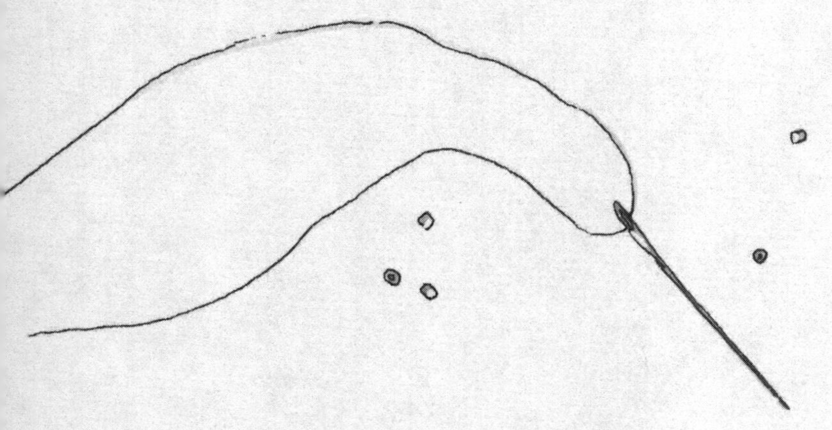

Kookoom, too, had much work to keep her busy. She had a small garden to look after, and fish and meat to smoke and dry on the racks set up outside.

She also had hides to tan, and plenty of sewing and beading to do. She had many grandchildren who wore the beautiful moccasins she sewed and decorated with dyed porcupine quills and beads.

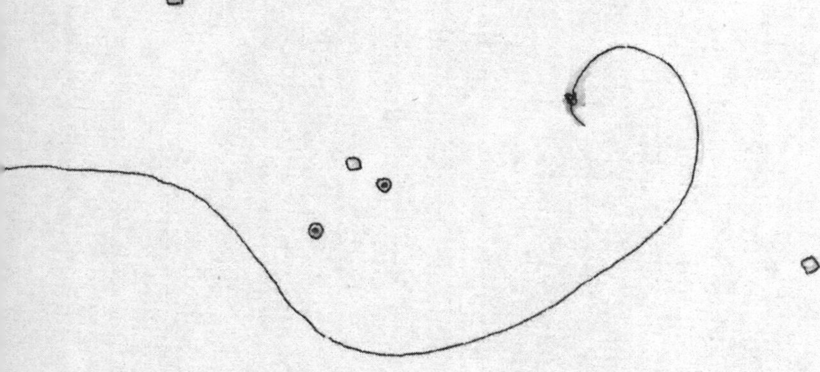

Ahsinee lived only ten miles from Mooshoom and Kookoom. For a little girl, it was like a million miles away.

She talked excitedly as she and her father bounced along the rough dirt road in the old pick-up truck. They arrived just as the sun was going down over the lake, the last rays casting a golden glow over the calm water.

Mooshoom's old dog, Ma-he-kun, limped out to meet them as they stopped in the yard. He wagged his tail in welcome.

There was a light in the kitchen window, and as Ahsinee jumped from the truck, she could smell freshly baked bannock and rabbit stew, which was her very favourite.

She had not realized she was so hungry.

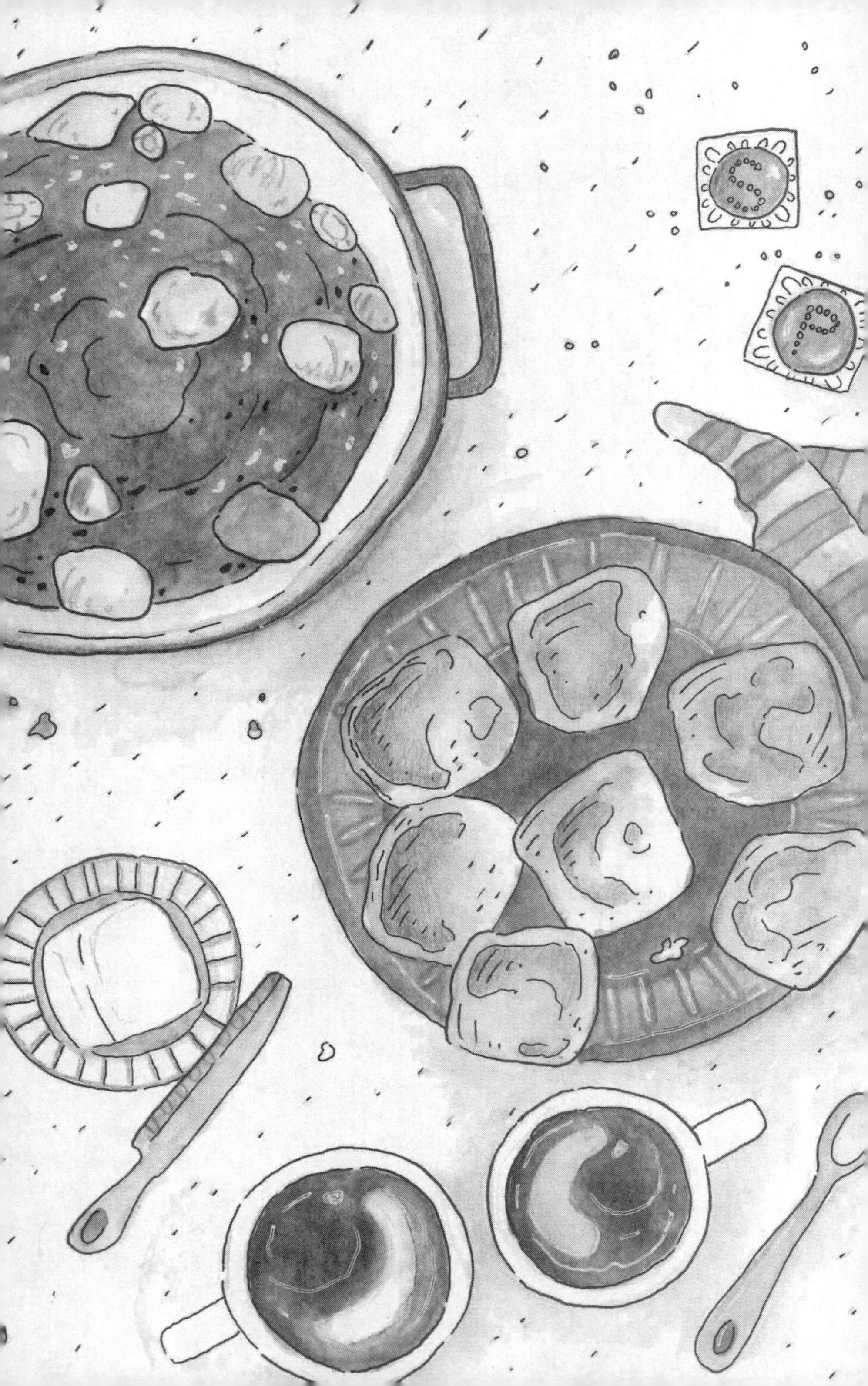

Kookoom bustled around the old black wood stove warming the stew and Bannock, which she served with steaming cups of tea.

Ahsinee sat down and ate and ate, until Mooshoom reminded her that Kookoom had baked some fresh Saskatoon pie.

Ahsinee was so full she could only smile and nod her head.

Yes, she had room for pie.

Soon they were all done and Kookoom got up to wash the dishes and clean the table.

This was the time of day that Ahsinee loved best.

It was always the same in the evening with the two old people. When Kookoom finished cleaning the supper dishes, she took her sewing to the table and began her work. Mooshoom built up the fire to take away the chill of evening.

Then he sat across from Kookoom to mend his nets. Kookoom smiled at Ahsinee because they both knew that Mooshoom would soon fall asleep.

Ahsinee sat between them, and after a time of silence, she would go to the cupboard where Mooshoom kept his pipe and tobacco.

Giving the pipe to the old man, she would ask for a story.

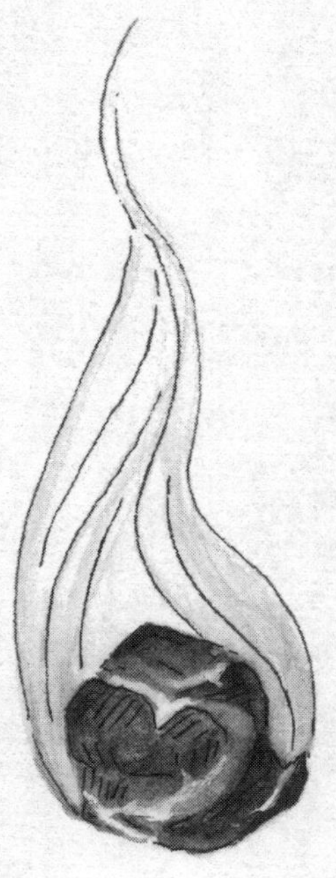

This evening Ahsinee could hardly wait.

She had something special to ask Mooshoom.

Maybe the old man would not have a story for this question, but Ahsinee rushed over to the cupboard for the pipe and tobacco.

In her hurry, she forgot old Ma-he-kun lying by the stove, and tripped over him. What a commotion! The old dog yelped so loudly that Mooshoom, who was sleeping soundly, woke up with a start.

Kookoom began to laugh.

"Waa-hi," said Mooshoom, as he helped Ahsinee up. "You must not always be in such a hurry. Here, sit down and rest before you get us all tired. We are old, remember, and our days of hurry are over."

Old Ma-he-kun growled in agreement.

Kookoom smiled as she bit the thread from the needle and said, "Speak for yourself and your dog, Old Man."

Mooshoom filled his pipe. As he packed the tobacco, he looked at Ahsinee.

"Your Kookoom makes jokes about my old bones. Pay her no mind for she has loved them for many years now."

Kookoom smiled and did not reply.

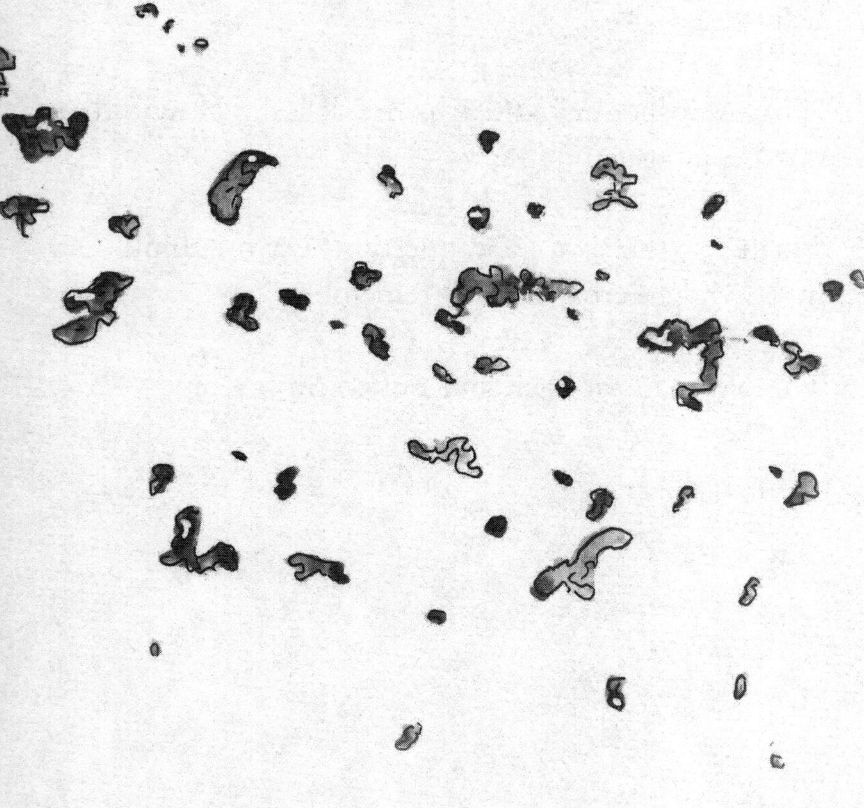

"Now, my girl," said Mooshoom, "what is it you want to know? It must be very important if you could not sit still for a moment and let your belly rest."

"Fire, Mooshoom," said Ahsinee at last. "How did our people get the fire?"

"Aaah . . . that is a good question. Let me think for a while. Perhaps I will remember."

The old man sat back and puffed on his pipe.

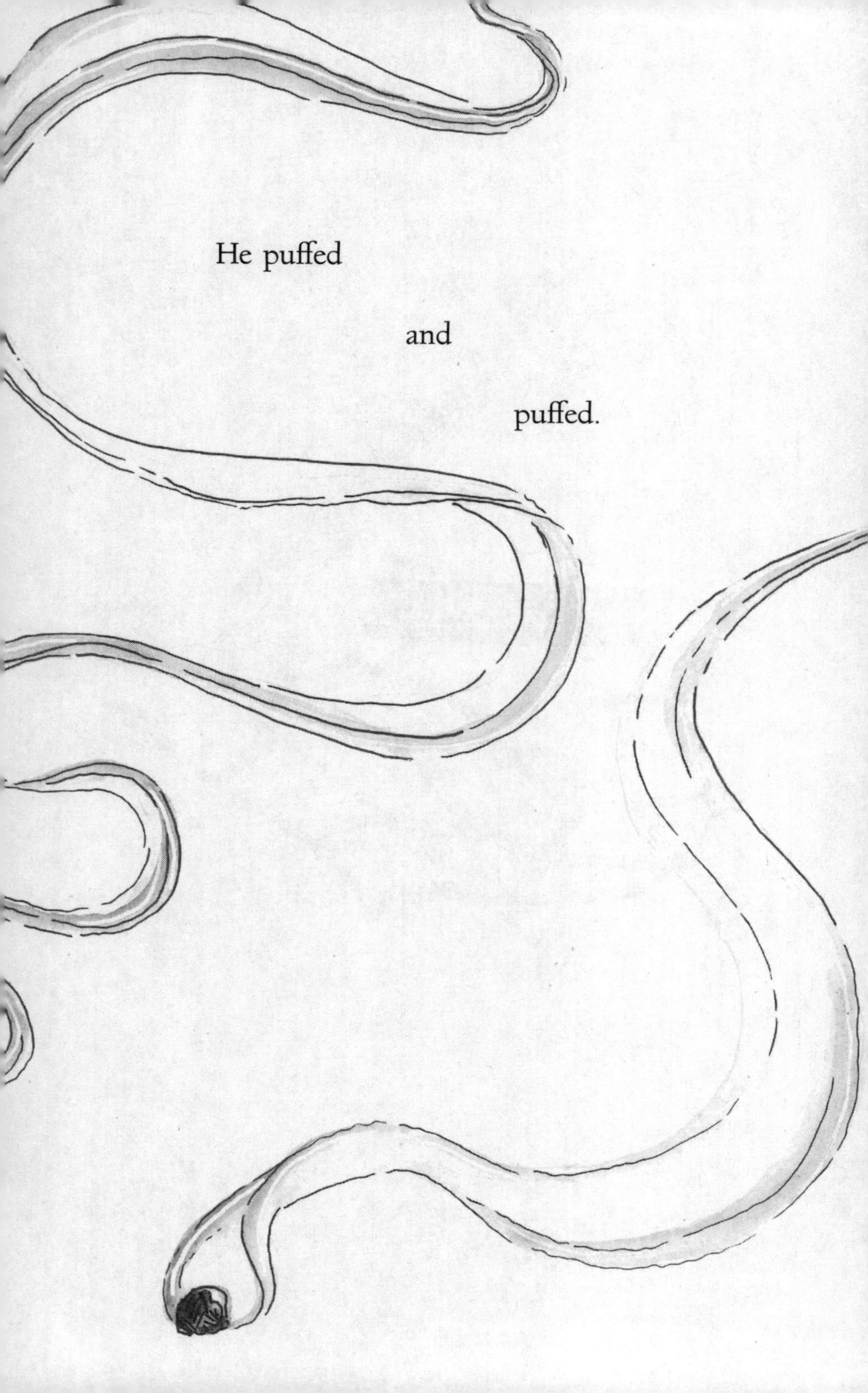

He puffed

and

puffed.

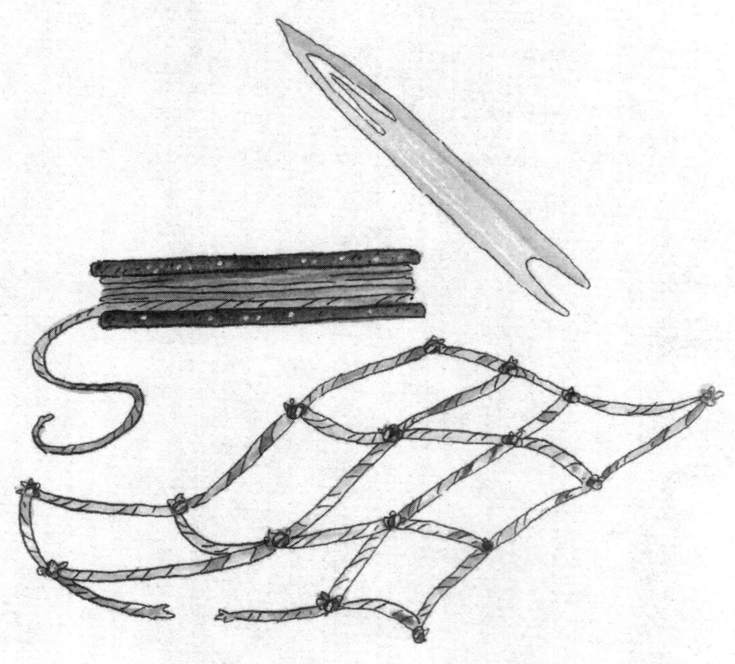

Finally he laid down his pipe and began to mend the net.

He worked for a long time, then he looked across at Kookoom.

"Do you remember the animal's name?"
he asked her.

Animal? Ahsinee looked at them. What did animals have to do with fire? Perhaps Mooshoom had forgotten.

"Mas-cha-can-is una," Kookoom replied.

"Aaah," interrupted Mooshoom, raising his hand. "Ni-kis-kis-in aqua, the Grey Coyote."

He took a big puff from his pipe and began to speak.

It was a long time ago when our mother, the earth, was young. In those days, people and animals all spoke one language. There was one animal who was a very good friend of the people and he often came to visit them. His name was Grey Coyote.

Now, Grey Coyote was a gentle and considerate creature. He was also very wise. When he visited, the people all gathered around and listened to him speak. Grey Coyote had one friend who was special, a boy named Little Badger.

Grey Coyote and Little Badger spent many hours talking. You see, Little Badger was blind. Grey Coyote took him on many long walks in the forest. He taught Little Badger about the earth he could not see, and how to smell, hear, and touch all the things around him.

He taught him that everything on the earth—human, animal, insect or plant—had a purpose.

This purpose was to serve and help each other.

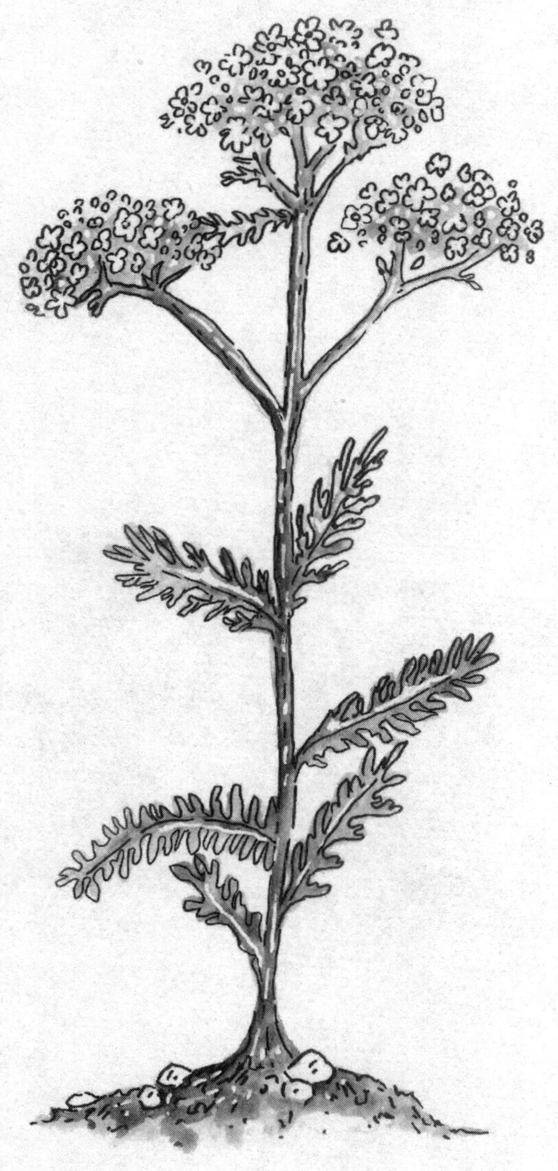

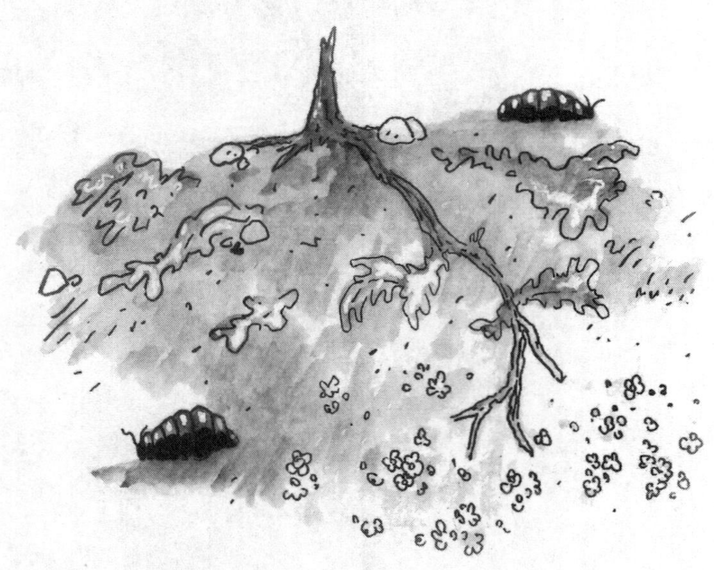

Little Badger's people lived in a world of plenty. Mother earth gave them all they needed. There was never any want.

However, with so much good, there had to be some bad.

For Little Badger's people, the bad was the long, cold winters. On winter days, the people took refuge in their teepees, huddled together for warmth.

One cold day, as Little Badger shivered under his robe, he thought: There must be some way for us to be warm. But how? Grey Coyote will know what to do. I will go and find him.

And he set off to find Grey Coyote.

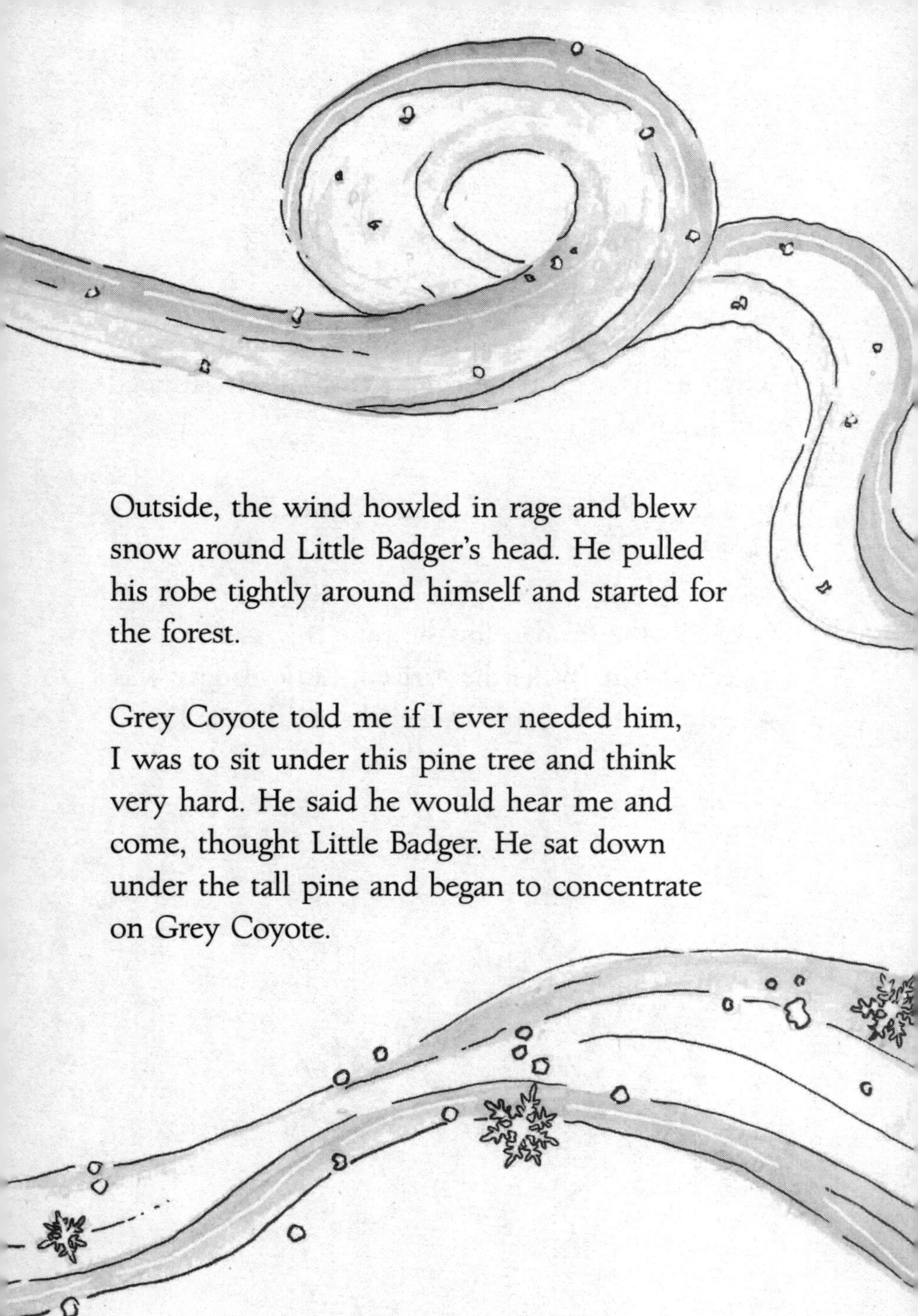

Outside, the wind howled in rage and blew snow around Little Badger's head. He pulled his robe tightly around himself and started for the forest.

Grey Coyote told me if I ever needed him, I was to sit under this pine tree and think very hard. He said he would hear me and come, thought Little Badger. He sat down under the tall pine and began to concentrate on Grey Coyote.

Grey Coyote was trotting through the forest when he heard a voice calling to him. He stopped and listened.

It is Little Badger, he thought. I must hurry. He sounds very weak.

Grey Coyote headed for the pine tree as fast as he could run. When he arrived, Little Badger was so cold his teeth rattled when he tried to talk.

“What is wrong, Little Brother?” asked Grey Coyote.

“My people are freezing to death,” chattered Little Badger. “You must help us.”

“How thoughtless of me,” said Grey Coyote. “I have a warm coat, and I never thought of my brothers and sisters. Here, I will shield you from the cold.” Grey Coyote wrapped himself around Little Badger.

"You must help us, Grey Coyote," Little Badger pleaded.

"You are wise. There must be some way for us to keep warm in the winter."

Grey Coyote thought and thought. Slowly he said,

"Yes, there is a way, Little Brother, but it is very dangerous."

"Tell me, Grey Coyote, before my people perish," cried Little Badger.

"There is a mountain far away from our land. Inside the mountain is fire. This fire is strange. It feeds on wood and rock and it burns forever. It would provide warmth for the people. But someone must go inside the mountain to get it."

"I will go," said Little Badger.

"Wait. I am not finished," warned Grey Coyote.

Inside the mountain lives the Fire Spirit. He has four strange creatures who stand guard for him.

"There is Mountain Goat who can stab you with his horns, Mountain Lion who can tear you apart with his claws, Grizzly Bear who can kill you with one slap of his mighty paw, and Rattlesnake whose teeth hold deadly poison.

And remember, Little Brother, you are blind and will not be able to see these dangers."

"I will still go," insisted Little Badger. "Will you take me to this place?"

Grey Coyote thought for a while.

"Yes, I will take you. Go back to your people. Find among them one hundred of the fastest runners. Bring them here tomorrow when the sun comes up."

"Where are you going?" asked Little Badger as Grey Coyote turned to leave.

"I am going to call the spirits to help us," said Grey Coyote as he trotted away.

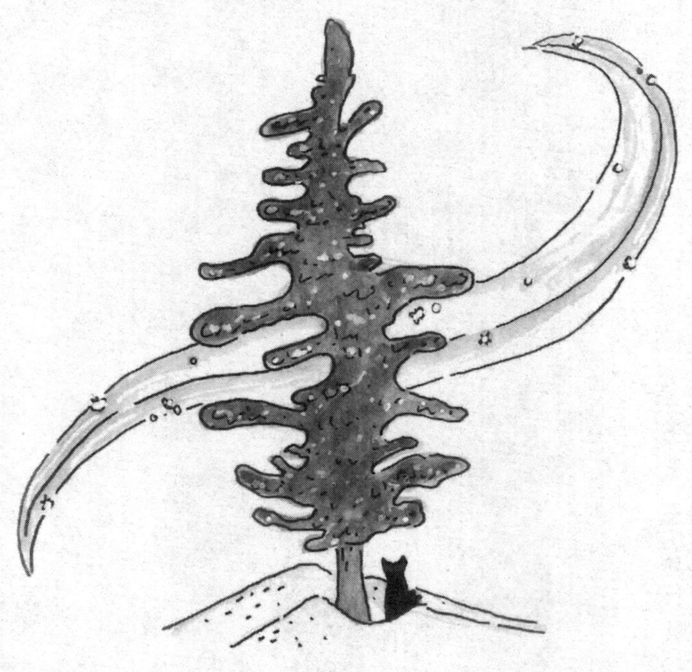

The next morning, when Little Badger met Grey Coyote by the pine tree, he had with him one hundred of the fastest runners and the wise men of the tribe. They held council, and the wise men asked the Great Spirit for strength, endurance, and courage for Little Badger, Grey Coyote, and the runners.

Then Grey Coyote spoke.

"I have talked to the spirits and they have given me guidance for our journey. They will do all in their power to help us reach the great mountain. Once we are there, Little Badger must go into the mountain alone. No power can help him until he has climbed back outside with the fire."

Now Grey Coyote said to the runners: "You must follow the direction in which I am pointing. That is where the mountain is."

He turned to the first runner. "You must run with Little Badger on your shoulders. When you have run as far as you can, the second runner will take Little Badger and do the same thing. You must wait where you are. When the last runner has gone as far as he can, I will meet him.

From there, Little Badger and I will go on alone.

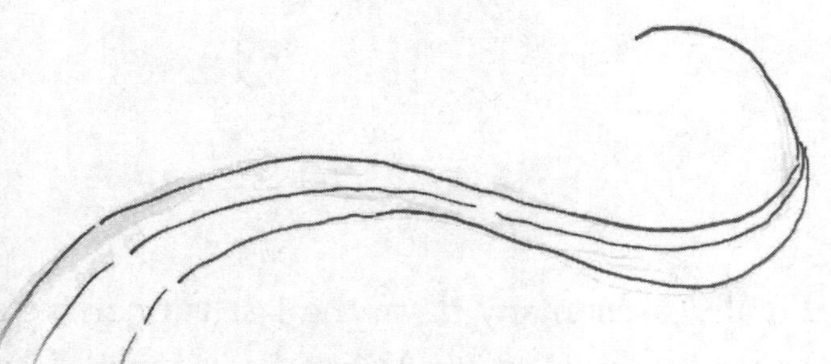

"I have told you of the journey there," continued Grey Coyote. "Now I will tell you of the journey back. Instead of carrying Little Badger, you will carry a stick of burning wood. You will bring it back here the same way you carried Little Badger. When you arrive here, the people of the tribe will feed the fire with small pieces of wood and keep it burning until Little Badger and I return."

The runners nodded and, picking up Little Badger, the first one started off. He ran so fast Little Badger felt he was flying through the air.

Finally, after many days, the last runner went as far as he could go. When he stopped, Grey Coyote appeared and led Little Badger to the foot of the mountain.

“Here is the mountain, Little Brother,” said Grey Coyote. “From here the spirits will guide and help you to the top. Once you reach the top, you must climb down the hole and get the fire yourself. When you have the fire and have climbed out, the spirits will help you down again. I will beat this drum and sing until you return.”

Little Badger took a deep breath. He was frightened, but he knew that if he failed, his people would continue to die from the cold.

He listened to the beat of the drum.

Suddenly, he did not feel frightened anymore and he began to climb.

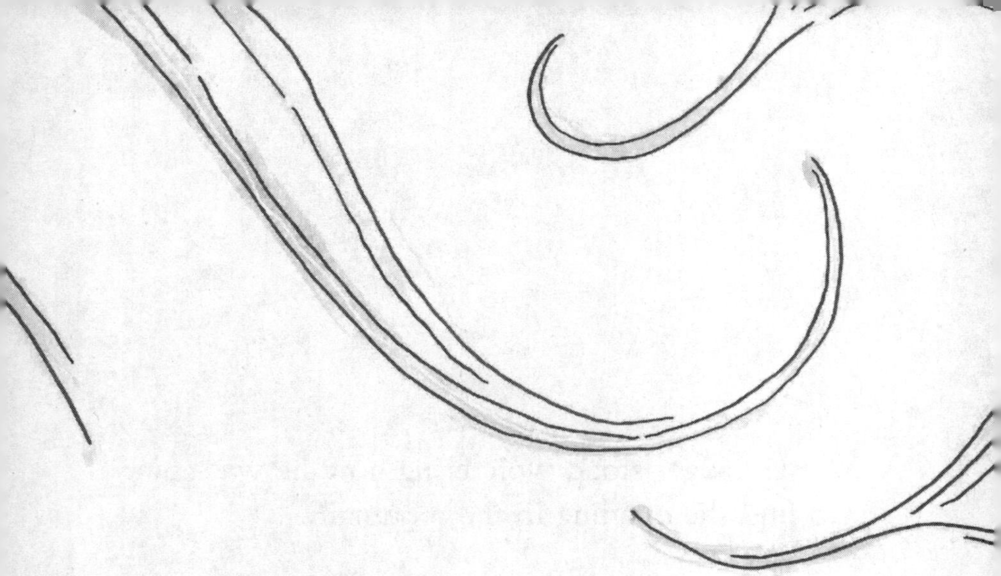

As he climbed, he felt the spirit of the wind steadying him, and the spirit of the rocks made the way smooth.

When he reached the top, he stopped to rest. He felt a last breath of air, then it was gone and he knew he was alone.

The spirits had left him.

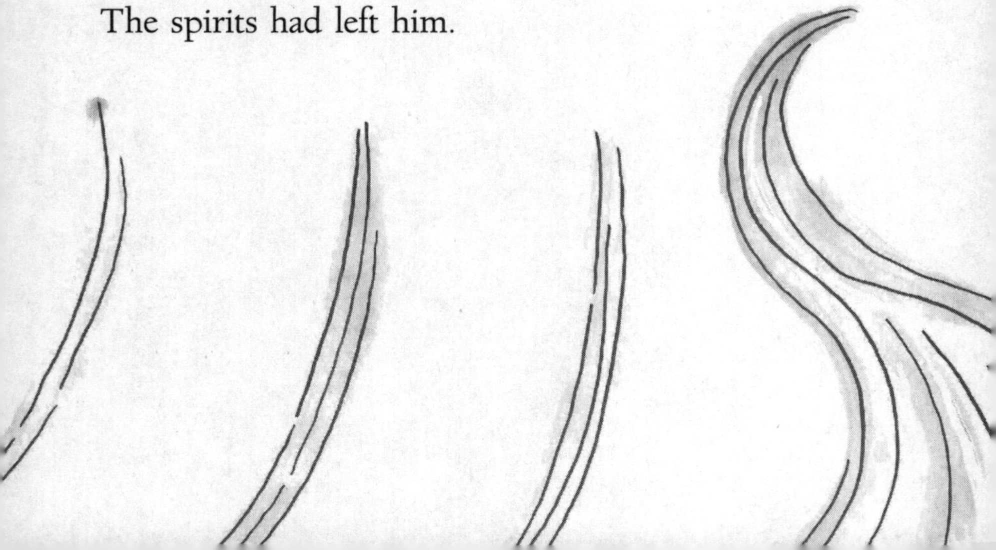

Little Badger stood wondering how he was going to find the opening in the mountain.

He began to move around slowly and to feel with his hands. A wave of warm air touched him and he knew he had found the entrance to the place of fire.

He stopped and listened for a moment. When he again heard the drum Grey Coyote was beating, he carefully started down.

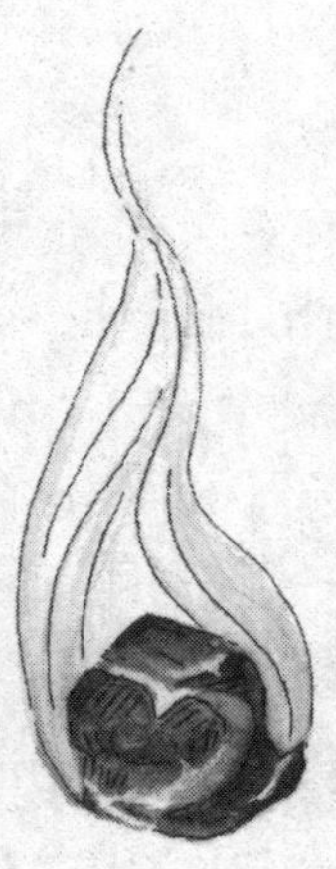

Suddenly, Little Badger heard a gruff voice:
"WHAT ARE YOU DOING HERE?
THIS PLACE IS FORBIDDEN TO YOU!"

Almost paralyzed with fear, he stayed very still. He knew he had come upon one of the guardians of the fire as it was told to him by Grey Coyote, but he did not know which one.

"I have come to see the Fire Spirit," he said, his voice shaking. "My people are cold and he is the only one who can help us."

"NO ONE CAN SEE THE FIRE SPIRIT,"
said the gruff voice.
"YOU CANNOT PASS BY ME.
IF YOU TRY, THEN I WILL KILL YOU."

Little Badger's heart pounded with fear. He had no weapons. He could not even see his enemy. As he clung to the rock ledge, he could hear Grey Coyote's drum beating. The sound comforted him, and his fear was gone. He reached out towards the voice. When he touched the creature, it trembled, and Little Badger could feel coarse hair.

"*WHY DO YOU DO THAT?*" grumbled the creature. "*NO ONE TOUCHES ME. MY HORNS COULD TEAR YOU APART.*" The words were angry, but the voice was frightened.

"Do not be afraid," said Little Badger gently. "I will not hurt you. As you can see, I have no weapons. I am blind. To know who you are, I must touch you. Ah, you are the Mountain Goat."

When Little Badger touched the Mountain Goat, he felt peace come over them. He told the creature of his mission.

The goat listened, then said, "*I WILL LET YOU GO BY, BUT I CANNOT HELP YOU GO BACK. BEWARE. THERE ARE THREE MORE GUARDIANS YOU MUST PASS BEFORE YOU REACH THE FIRE SPIRIT. I WISH YOU GOOD FORTUNE, LITTLE BROTHER.*"

Little Badger continued climbing down inside of the mountain. As he descended, he could feel the heat of the fire. When he heard a soft growl, he knew he had met the Mountain Lion.

Little Badger reached out and touched the animal. As he stroked the smooth fur, he told the Lion of his people. They could hear the drum far off in the distance and again peace settled over both of them.

The Lion growled softly, "*YOU MAY GO ON.*"

Little Badger continued his slow climb down. He knew he still had to meet the Grizzly Bear and the Rattlesnake, but he was no longer afraid. If things went on as they had, he knew he would make two new friends.

It was true. When he met the Grizzly Bear and touched him, they became friends. The Bear warned him that the Rattlesnake was very dangerous.

"YOU MUST BE VERY CAREFUL, LITTLE BROTHER," he rumbled in his great voice, as the boy turned to go. *"YOU MUST USE WISDOM TO GET BY RATTLER, FOR HIS MEDICINE IS VERY POWERFUL."*

Little Badger continued his climb down towards the fire. Soon he met the Rattlesnake. The Snake coiled, rattled his tail and raised his mighty head up to strike.

When Little Badger heard the sound of the rattle, he quickly said, "You must be the Snake. What a beautiful rattle you have."

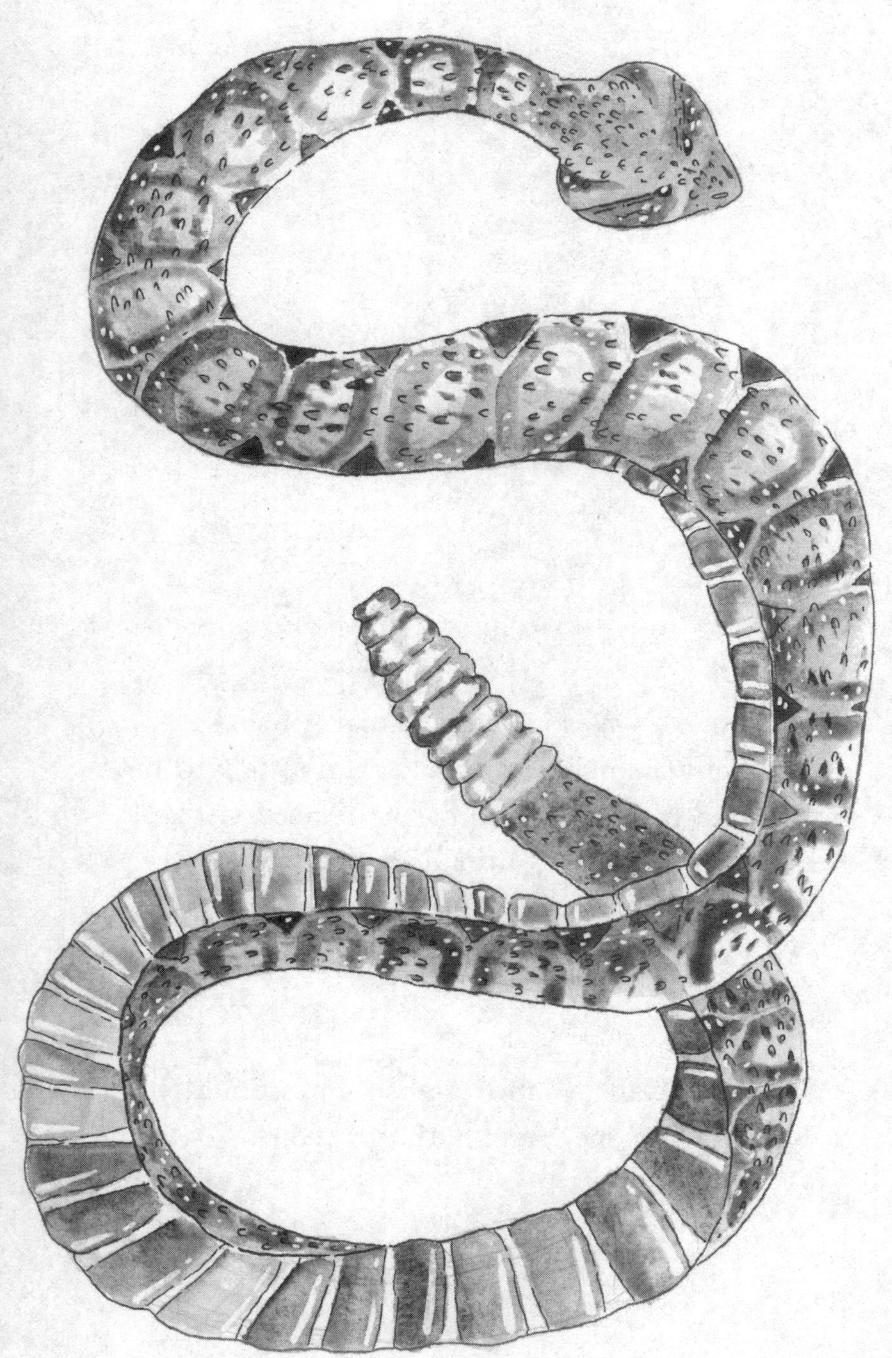

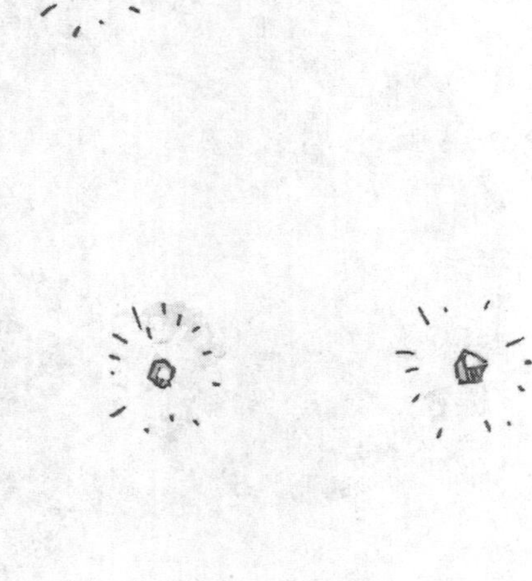

Rattlesnake was so surprised that someone, especially a small boy, would dare to talk to him, and find him beautiful, that he relaxed without even realizing he had done so.

"*WHY ARE YOU NOT AFRAID OF ME?*" he hissed.

"I do not want to hurt you, so why should you want to hurt me?" replied Little Badger.

Rattlesnake was astonished at the little boy's words. He was thinking about what the boy had said and did not notice him leave to continue his climb.

Little Badger had almost finished his journey to meet the Fire Spirit. It was so hot, he felt his braids must be singed. He was also very tired and he stumbled.

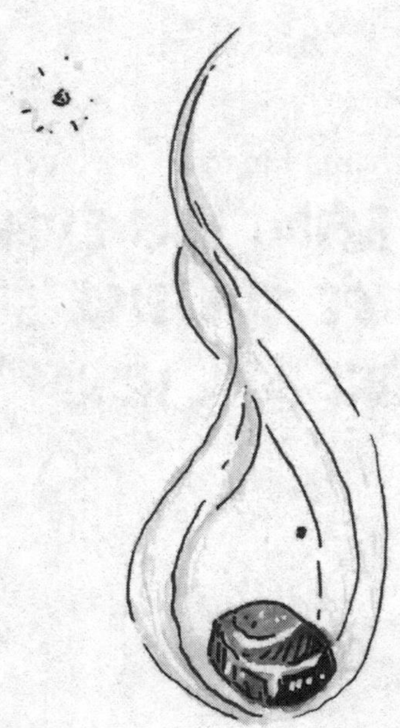

As he tried to catch his balance, a voice crackled,

"NO HUMAN BEING HAS EVER SEEN THE HOME OF THE FIRE SPIRIT. WHY ARE YOU HERE?"

Little Badger knew that at last he had met the Fire Spirit.

“I cannot see your home,” replied Little Badger, “for I am blind. It is very warm. If my people lived here, they would never be cold.”

"COLD? COLD?"
said the Fire Spirit.
"WHAT IS COLD?"

As he talked, he flamed up and all the colours of the rainbow seemed to glow around him.

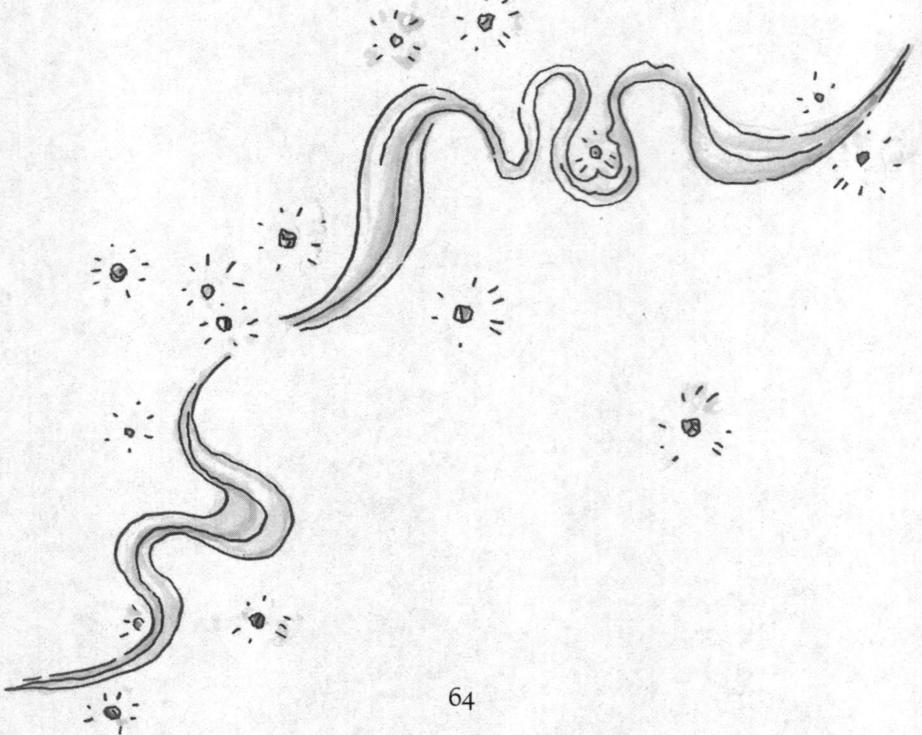

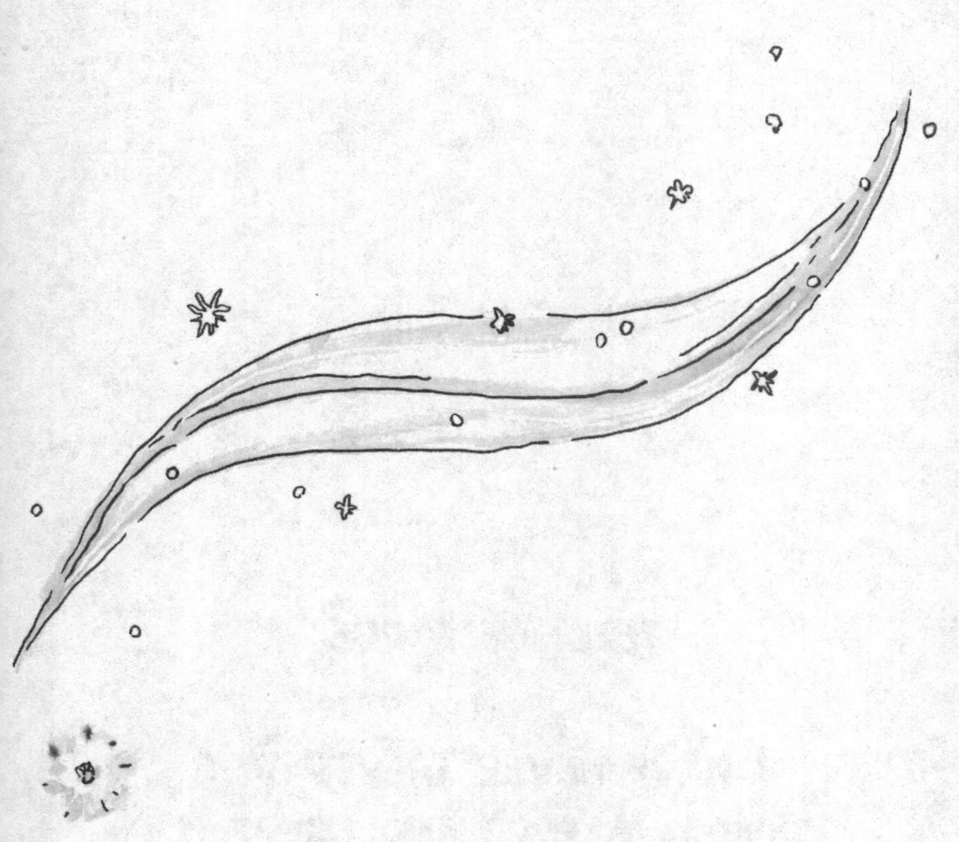

Little Badger could not see the flames but he felt a gust of warm air as the Spirit spoke.

"When the snows come," explained Little Badger, "my people are very cold. There is not enough warmth from the sun, so many of them die. I have come to ask you for fire to warm my people."

"TELL ME MORE,"

said the Fire Spirit.

"I HAVE NEVER TALKED TO A HUMAN BEFORE AND THERE IS MUCH I DO NOT KNOW."

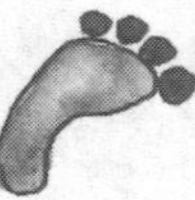

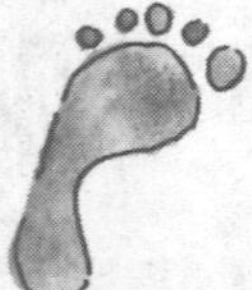

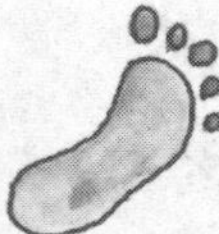

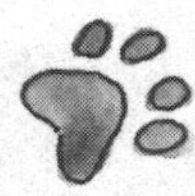

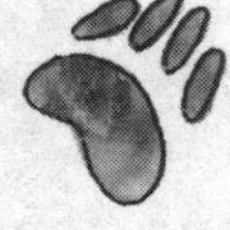

Little Badger sat down. He told the Fire Spirit about his land and his people. He told of his journey into the heart of the mountain and of the friends he had made along the way.

The Fire Spirit was quiet for a long time. All that Little Badger could hear was the hiss of his flames.

Finally the Spirit spoke:

"HOW LONG HAVE YOU BEEN BLIND?"

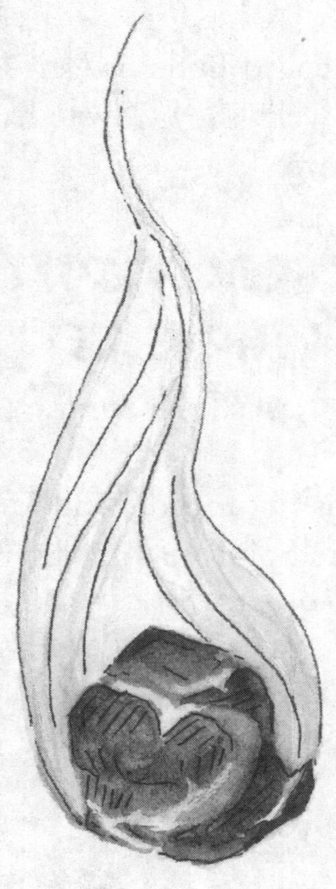

"All my life," replied Little Badger. "But I can feel and hear very well. Grey Coyote has taught me. He is like my eyes."

**"GREY COYOTE?
WHO IS HE?"**

asked the Spirit.

"Grey Coyote is my friend," said Little Badger. He told the Fire Spirit how his friend had taught him about the world.

"He brought me to this mountain and he is waiting for me now. Listen. Can you hear him? He is beating a drum."

The Fire Spirit listened.

"YES, I CAN HEAR HIM,"

he replied.

"The drum gave me courage and strength," said Little Badger. "It helped me make new friends."

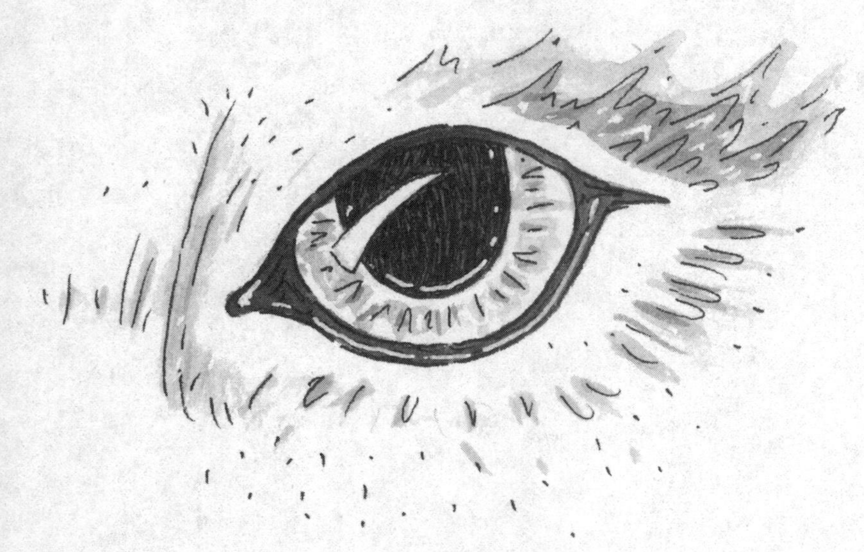

Little Badger and the Fire Spirit sat together for a long time and listened to the faint beating of the drum.

"IT IS STRONG AND BEAUTIFUL MUSIC,"

said the Fire Spirit.

"I WILL NEVER FORGET IT.... HERE, TAKE THIS BURNING STICK. IT IS THE WARMTH OF FRIENDSHIP THAT YOU BROUGHT TO THIS PLACE. IT WILL KEEP YOUR PEOPLE WARM FOREVER."

Little Badger was bursting with gratitude.

"DO NOT THANK ME FOR IT, LITTLE BROTHER. YOU SHARED YOUR WARMTH WITH ME, AND I WILL SHARE MINE WITH YOU. WHEN YOU REACH THE TOP OF THE MOUNTAIN, YOU WILL NO LONGER BE BLIND. YOU WILL SEE THE WORLD THAT YOUR FRIEND, GREY COYOTE, HAS TAUGHT YOU ABOUT. GO NOW, HE WAITS FOR YOU."

Little Badger took the stick, said goodbye to the Fire Spirit and began to climb up out of the mountain. As he climbed, he met his friends and said goodbye to them also.

When he reached the top, with the stick of fire in his hand, he saw a great light.

He saw the world for the first time in his life.

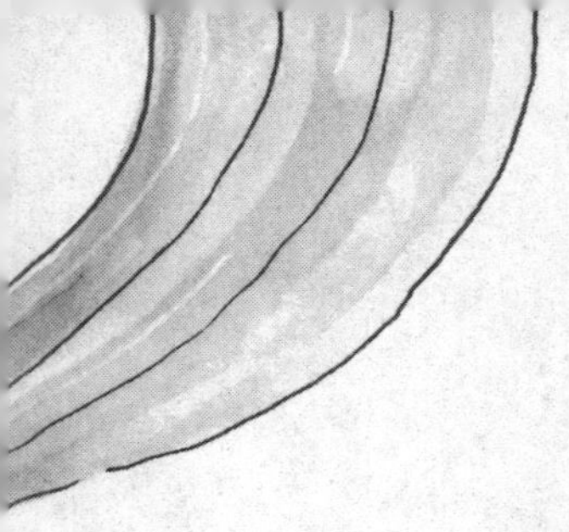

He stopped for a long time and looked and looked at the world. It was so beautiful. His eyes filled with tears of happiness. He felt the Spirit of the wind touch his hair gently and whisper, "Listen, Little Brother."

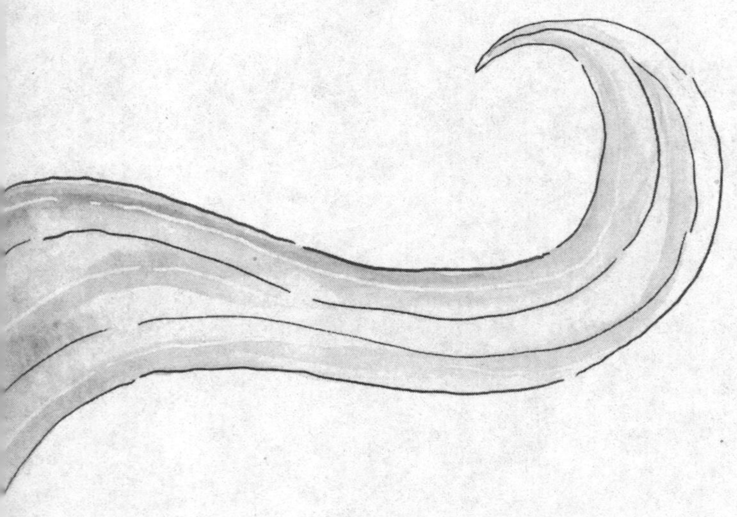

From far below, at the foot of the mountain, came the beating of the drum. As Little Badger listened, he heard two drums, then three.

How can there be three drums? he wondered.

He listened again. Now there were four, five, then six drums. Soon the air was filled with the sound of many drums, all of different sizes, making different and beautiful sounds.

Suddenly Little Badger smiled. He knew Grey Coyote's magic drum was his heartbeat. The other drums were the beating hearts of all living things.

Little Badger
laughed as he
climbed down
the mountain.

Around him was
the sound of the
drums, the pulse
of the world,
the music of
the universe.

The story was finished, and Ahsinee's eyes were shining as she said, "Oh, Mooshoom, it was a beautiful story. But what happened to the fire?"

Mooshoom struck a match to light his pipe, then answered her.

"Little Badger brought the fire home to his people, and we have it to this day."

"Tell me another story about Little Badger," Ahsinee pleaded.

"It is time for bed, my girl," Kookoom said. "There will be many more stories later. We have all summer, remember."

Ahsinee could hear a loon calling from across the lake as she snuggled down in the soft feather bed.

Yes, they had all summer together, and Mooshoom and Kookoom had so many stories to tell.

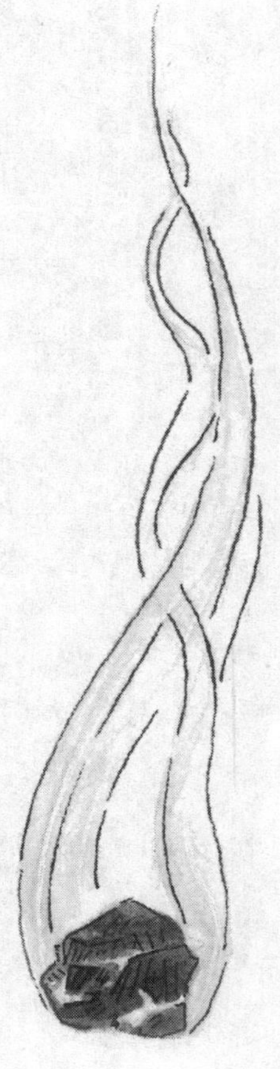

MARIA CAMPBELL is a Métis writer, playwright, filmmaker, scholar, teacher, community organizer, activist, and elder (born April 26, 1939, in Park Valley, Saskatchewan). Campbell's memoir *Halfbreed* (1973) is regarded as a foundational work of Indigenous literature in Canada. She has authored several other books and plays, and has directed and written scripts for a number of films. She has also worked with Indigenous youth in community theatre and advocated for the hiring and recognition of Indigenous people in the arts. She has mentored many Indigenous artists during her career, co-established shelters for Indigenous women and children, and run a cultural centre at Gabriel's Crossing.

Campbell is the winner of the 2023 Cheryl and Henry Kloppenburg Award for Literary Excellence, was named a fellow of the Pierre Elliott Trudeau Foundation in 2012, was appointed to the Stanley Knowles Distinguished Visiting Professorship at Brandon University, and has served as Cultural Advisor at the University of Saskatchewan College of Law and Gwenna Moss Centre for Teaching since 2017. She is an officer of the Order of Canada and holds eight honorary doctorates.

A NOTE ABOUT THE ART

The art on the cover and interior of this book is by Métis artist Kate Boyer, of St. Laurent, Saskatchewan. "I love art! Ever since I got in trouble for scribbling a unicorn into a book about Canadian landscapes I've been hooked. To me, making art is my own little way of making magic. Art should bring joy and be accessible to everyone and should make you want to grab a pencil and create a whole new world on a fresh page, a sneaker, or even a wall! In this book, I tried to create images that resemble real things but also have a playfulness about them that makes you want to tell your own story. As well, the contrast between the white of the page and the black of the lines could make a perfect colouring page . . . (don't tell the publisher I said that)." Boyer has worked on children's book illustrations, commissions, set designs, short films, and much more. When she's not making art she enjoys parkour, skateboarding, and curling up to watch movies with her partner and her cat.

A NOTE ABOUT THE TYPE

The text is set in Village, designed in 1903 by Frederic Goudy. Village was the first of many book faces that Goudy would design, and was used for his printing company, The Village Press. David Berlow revived and updated the font in the 1990s, expanding the number of styles to make it a complete type family.

Kanata is an Iroquois word meaning "village," so it seems an apt typeface in which to set this classics series.

THE KANATA CLASSICS SERIES

NISHGA by Jordan Abel

CHILDHOOD by André Alexis

THIS WOUND IS A WORLD by Billy-Ray Belcourt

HALFBREED by Maria Campbell

LITTLE BADGER AND THE FIRE SPIRIT by Maria Campbell

AMERICAN WAR by Omar El Akkad

BEAR by Marian Engel

ISLAND by Alistair MacLeod

THE TIN FLUTE by Gabrielle Roy

RU by Kim Thúy

MEDICINE WALK by Richard Wagamese

STARLIGHT by Richard Wagamese